Patriots of African Descent In the Revolutionary War

Part 1

By

Marion T. Lane

Illustrated by the Kalpart team

The Elevator Group
Paoli, Pennsylvania

Patriots of African Descent in the Revolutionary War, Part 1, by Marion T. Lane

Copyright ©2011 by Marion T. Lane

Book Design/Layout, Illustrations and Book Cover design by The Kalpart Team

Publisher: The Elevator Group, PO Box 207, Paoli, PA 19301

www.TheElevatorGroup.com info@TheElevatorGroup.com

Paperback ISBN: 978-0-9824945-4-7 LCCN: 2011945737

(Previously published in a hardcover version by Strategic Book Group with ISBN 978-1-60976-517-0)

To order additional copies or to order bulk copies at a discount, please contact the publisher, The Elevator Group, as noted above.

Manufactured by:

Color House Graphics, Inc., Grand Rapids, MI USA

October 2013

Job #41071

This work is dedicated to my father who has provided guidance, patience and support for my every step along life's path.

M.L.

Table of Contents

Chapter 1 - The Topic

As Jeremy traveled home from school, he was thinking a lot about what had been discussed in his social studies class. Jeremy attends the Dunlap Elementary School in Philadelphia. His fifth-grade teacher, Mrs. Woods, began discussing a new topic that day and he just could not stop thinking about it.

The topic for the next social studies unit was going to be the Revolutionary War. Mrs. Woods told the class they would learn about many battles, various heroes, and how the war was won.

Jeremy loved history. He remembered from fourth grade learning about the colonists coming from Europe and settling in the Northeast and Southeast areas. He remembered learning about the American Indians, slaves and the colonists. He began to wonder who the people were that participated in the Revolutionary War.

That night, during dinner, Jeremy decided to ask his Pop-Pop if he knew about the Revolutionary War. Pop-Pop was eighty-six years old and knew about many things. His Pop-Pop stopped eating, sat back in the chair, and smiled at Jeremy. He was very pleased that

Jeremy had asked this question and was interested in the Revolution.

Finally, Pop-Pop answered, "Yes Jeremy, I know quite a lot about the Revolutionary War. What would you like to know?"

Jeremy responded by asking, "Who were the heroes? Where did the war take place? Were there black people in the war?"

Pop-Pop was so happy and proud that his great-grandson was asking these questions. Pop-Pop recognized Jeremy was now ready to be told some important information. "After we finish eating, I want you to come upstairs to my study and I will answer your questions," Pop-Pop told Jeremy.

Chapter 2 - Colonial Times

Later that evening, Jeremy joined Pop-Pop in his study. Jeremy loved Pop-Pop's study with the big desk and chair. There were lots of books and the biggest dictionary he had ever seen on a stand against the wall. He could never lift it. It must have weighed fifty pounds.

As Pop-Pop opened the desk, Jeremy was wondering what could be in the leather binder he removed from the bottom drawer. Pop-Pop always kept his desk locked because his most important papers were stored there.

Placing the binder on the top of the desk, Pop-Pop paused and asked Jeremy, "What facts have you learned about the colonies?" Jeremy quickly replied that last year while in Mrs. Johnson's fourth-grade class, he learned that thirteen years before the Pilgrims landed at Plymouth,

Massachusetts on the Mayflower, 104 English settlers arrived at Jamestown Island in Virginia on May 14, 1607. Altogether, there were thirteen original colonies, spread from Maine to Georgia. Many of the original colonists were rich people who brought their indentured servants with them. Although the British were the first to establish a colony, later Holland, Sweden, France, and Spain did.

Indentured servants were generally poor people who worked for someone, under a contract, for up to seven years and then they were free to do what they wanted. Many times they were given land as payment for their services and they became farmers. Sometimes they purchased land with their earnings. The colonists did not like hard labor and had a difficult time getting along with the Indians. Therefore, some returned to Europe.

He also knew the first documented Africans arrived in Virginia in 1619 from the kingdom of Angola, and they were not slaves. The first Africans had been captured by the Dutch during a conflict with the Portuguese. When they arrived, they were treated as indentured servants. It wasn't until around 1641 that the practice of owning Africans as slaves for life came to be. Slavery was first legalized in Massachusetts around this time.

In 1676, Africans who had become slaves, African indentured servants, and British indentured servants joined together and participated in Bacon's Rebellion against the Indians.

Chapter 3 - Intolerance

Pop-Pop was very impressed by what Jeremy knew. "Well Jeremy, you certainly have learned a lot of information."

"I love history," Jeremy responded.

"Let me pick up the story following the colonists' successful stand during Bacon's Rebellion," Pop-Pop commented. He began by saying that during this next period of time, the African and British indentured servants shared many experiences of life and some were respected by the colonists. This alliance was seen in their stand with the British against the French and Native Americans in the seven-year French and Indian War. This war took place between 1754 and 1763. The British defeated the French. However, the colonists, the indentured servants, and slaves learned how to fight. They learned how to use weapons and realized that they no longer needed the British Army for protection. They were now not afraid of the French or the British.

The king of England attempted to keep control of the colonists by passing laws, especially tax laws. In 1765, the British passed the Stamp Act on paper or parchment. In 1767, when the British passed the Townshend Act to place taxes on tea, glass, paper, and paint, the colonists became very angry. They felt it was not fair for them to be taxed without having representation in the British Parliament—"taxation without representation." They refused to pay these taxes or buy any goods made in England.

Because the colonists would not pay, the king sent approximately 40,000 soldiers to help the tax collectors. Also, the colonists were told the soldiers had to live in their homes. Now, they were really, really angry.

On March 5, 1770, a small group of colonists in Boston were bullying, calling names, and throwing stones at some British soldiers. They did this quite often. A soldier fired several shots from his musket into the crowd leaving a runaway slave, Crispus Attucks, and four others dead. This event became known as the Boston Massacre. Crispus Attucks, twenty-seven years old and the son of an African father and Indian mother, was one of the first persons to die for the cause of the American Revolution.

The colonists wanted independence. A short time later in 1773, a group of fifty colonists in Boston disguised themselves by dressing up as Indians and in the dark of the night boarded three ships docked at Griffin's Wharf. They boarded them even though the three ships were surrounded by British armed ships of war. The ships contained 342 crates of tea. The disguised colonists opened the crates and threw the contents overboard into the ocean.

The king really wanted to punish the colonists, so he created the Intolerable Acts, which closed Boston Harbor until the tea was paid for. As a result, the people could not receive food via ships. The other colonies sent food to them over land.

Chapter 4 - The Continental Forces

Next, all the colonies except Georgia sent representatives to Philadelphia to decide what to do. In September 1774, they met in Carpenter's Hall. This group meeting was called the First Continental Congress. At the meeting, it was decided to cut off trade with England until the British changed the Intolerable Acts.

Some colonists began arming themselves and preparing to fight. They practiced responding to have to fight at a minute's notice; hence, they were nicknamed "the Minutemen."

In April 1775, the British commander in Boston sent soldiers to Concord, Massachusetts to look for their guns and gunpowder. He wanted his soldiers to take away the colonists' guns and gunpowder. A man named

Paul Revere rode all night on horseback to Lexington, Massachusetts to warn the colonists. This was called the "midnight ride of Paul Revere."

The next day, the British soldiers and the colonists clashed. The first shot of the Battle of Lexington and Concord is referred to as "the shot heard around the world" because the war was on.

It was time for the representatives to meet again. Therefore, the Second Continental Congress met in Philadelphia in May of 1775.

During this meeting, the colonies that had not started fighting were asked to provide supplies and soldiers. They decided to ask France to help them and appointed George Washington as Commander-in-Chief of the army.

Well, if you thought the king was angry before, now he was angry with a capital "A." So what did he do? He hired soldiers, the Hessians, from the western part of Germany to help the British.

In 1656, the colony of Massachusetts excluded the Africans and Indians from the militia. However, it was now time to debate this policy. By 1775, the Africans were called Negroes. Massachusetts decided to keep its policy, but the other colonies did not feel the same way because the slave and indentured servants had helped in the other colonial conflicts.

George Washington looking at a picture of King George

"Yes!" said Jeremy. "They helped in Bacon's Rebellion and the French and Indian War."

By the fall of 1775, the debate escalated whether "Negroes" should be enlisted in George Washington's army. Georgia, which now had sent delegates to the Continental Congress, expressed fears for the safety of Georgia and South Carolina. They were afraid of the British offering freedom to all Negroes willing to be loyal to the king and fight with the British. The delegates from Georgia knew the slaves had a skill of communicating among themselves as to convey information several hundred miles in a week or a fortnight (two weeks).

George Washington had been informed that the free Negroes in Massachusetts were very displeased at being excluded from enlistment. Fearing they might join the enemy and considering the concerns of the delegates from Georgia and others, Washington departed from the exclusion policy for his Continental Army. As a result, a number of slaves and indentured servants joined the regiments. In fact, over 5,000 black men served on the Continental Line in the Revolution.

Pop-Pop continued, "You must know Indians also enlisted. These men served in the various state militias and in the Continental Army where they were sailors, infantrymen, and cavaliers. They are called patriots. Let me clarify, that some black men also joined with the British, the Hessians, and the Loyalists."

"Wow!" said Jeremy.

Pop-Pop went on to clarify that many of these men served as privateers or enlisted as freedmen. A great many slaves were freed before and others after they served. Some slaves acted as substitutes for their masters in the regiments. From the beginning of the war, they stood side by side with the colonists using weapons, being killed, and distinguishing themselves as heroes. For example, before the officials could decide whether or not to allow black men to join, Peter Salem, a free Negro, killed the British Major Pitcairn at the Battle of Bunker Hill in Massachusetts.

Chapter 5 - Our Family

Jeremy asked his great-grandfather how he came to know all of this information. His great-grandfather explained that their family had been involved in the Revolutionary War. "Really!" exclaimed Jeremy.

Just then, someone called Jeremy's name. The sound was coming from downstairs. "Jeremy! Jeremy!" The voice was that of his mother.

"Yes!" Jeremy responded. She told him it was time for his bath and to get ready for bed. "Oh no!" cried Jeremy. The story was too good to stop now. Jeremy ran downstairs and pleaded with his mother. He reminded her it was Friday and he had received an "A" on both his math and spelling tests at school that day. She relented, giving him an additional thirty minutes before starting his bath.

His great-grandfather informed Jeremy that their family originally came from a place near Jamestown called Charles City County, Virginia. Records indicate they had been indentured servants, who were later referred to as freedmen. "These family members were our ancestors," said Pop-Pop.

One of the earliest was Elizabeth Brown, born around 1722 as an indentured servant. She was thought to be a third generation New World indentured servant. She was referred to as "mulatto," meaning she was not of a dark complexion. The British indentured servants, the African indentured servants, and by now the Indians socialized together, often having common-law marriages.

It is believed Elizabeth Brown had eight sons: John, born 1739; Abraham, born 1741; Edward, born 1742; William, born 1743; Dixon, born 1745; Freeman, born 1748; Benjamin, born 1755; and Isaac, born 1760.

It has been documented that at least three of her sons were "bound out." In other words, they received pay

for court-ordered service. The court ordered the church wardens to bind out her sons John, Abraham, and Will Brown to Jacob Danzee.

"We are direct descendants of both Abraham Brown and Isaac Brown," said Pop-Pop. "I will explain more about how that came to be later."

While Elizabeth lived and raised her children in Charles City County, the government of Virginia was under British control. Records indicate Abraham, the second of Elizabeth's eight sons, purchased 156 acres of land in Westover Parish, Charles City County on September 27, 1769 for ninety-six pounds.

Chapter 6 - Duncastle's Ordinary

In 1775, Lord Dunmore was the British governor. In March of 1775, there was a call for the organization of a cavalry or infantry in every county in Virginia during the Second Continental Congress. Hearing of this, Lord Dunmore ordered his royal marines to secretly remove fifteen half barrels of gunpowder from the public warehouse, called a magazine, in the capital, Williamsburg.

Next, Lord Dunmore threatened to free the colony's slaves. This greatly upset the plantation owners and increased opposition to the king. There were lots of plantations in Virginia by this time.

Taking the initiative, Patrick Henry from Hanover County and John Tyler from Charles City County collected troops and marched to Duncastle's Ordinary, which was sixteen miles from Williamsburg. A frightened

Lord Dunmore sent a bill of exchange for the value of the gunpowder. In other words, he arranged to pay for it.

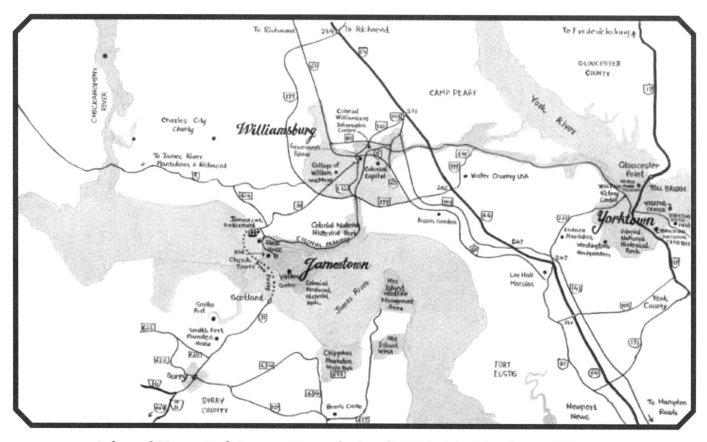

Atlas of Historical County Boundaries (2000). The Newberry Library.
Retrieved January 6, 2011, from historical- county.newberry.org/Virginia/viewer.htm

A Virginia convention met and passed an ordinance dividing the colony into military districts. The deputies of the convention authorized the formation of a Minuteman battalion. They assigned commissions of "captain" to several people.

John Tyler was confirmed as captain of the company of troops he had previously organized. The deputies

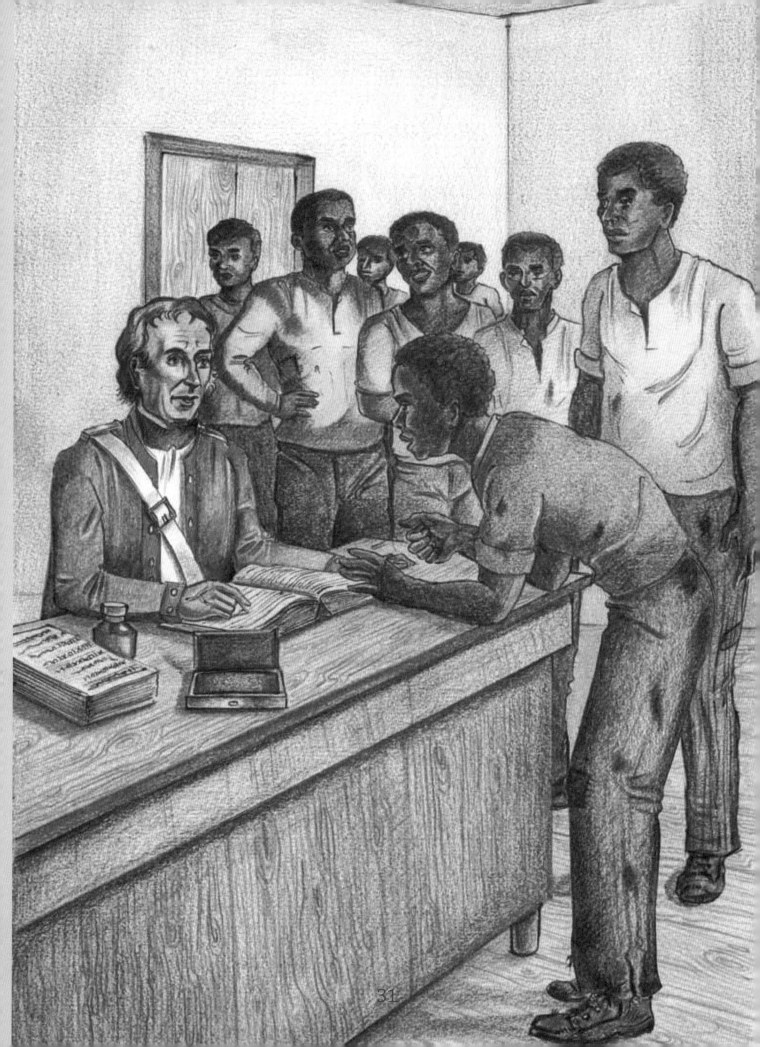

wanted to show that the authority to raise troops and grant commissions would rest solely with government officials. By the way, Tyler was the father of the man who became the tenth President of the United States, John Tyler, Jr.

In November 1775, Lord Dunmore delivered on his threat to free the slaves because he was badly in need of able-bodied men. He issued a proclamation declaring, "All indented servants, Negroes, or others, (appertaining to Rebels,) free that are able and willing to bear arms, they joining His Majesty's troops as soon as may be, for the more speedily reducing this colony to a proper sense of their duty, to His Majesty's crown and dignity."

Although the governor was able to recruit approximately five hundred blacks, the full-scale rush to join his troops that he envisioned did not happen.

The slave owners were spreading the word that the British would ship them to the West Indies after the war. The slaves actually hoped they would gain freedom and liberty after their masters gained theirs. This was a logical conclusion because they saw how much the principles of freedom and liberty meant to the colonists.

On the evening of July 4, 1776, the Continental Congress signed the Declaration of Independence. John Hancock, the president of the Congress, signed

the document in bold letters. This act represented the colonies official break from England.

Lord Dunmore finally fled Virginia, sailing to New York in August of 1776 with three hundred black Virginians on board. The others died due to a fever epidemic.

Many free Negroes enlisted and so many slaves deserted their masters for the army that the state, in 1777, enacted a law providing that no Negro should be enlisted unless he had a certificate of freedom.

Chapter 7 - The Interruption

"Jeremy! Jeremy!" Jeremy knew he had to prepare to get his bath and go to bed now.

"Okay Mom," he responded. Pop-Pop had not opened the leather binder yet. Pop-Pop told Jeremy that they would continue the story the next day after breakfast and after Jeremy finished his chores. Jeremy wondered what was in the binder so he asked about it. Pop-Pop said he would see the items in the morning.

As Jeremy prepared for bed, he had visions of all the things his great-grandfather had shared. He felt so excited and proud to find out there had been patriots in his own family. He could have never imagined that in a million years.

The next day was a Saturday. Jeremy got up early and ate his breakfast. He then went upstairs and changed the sheets on his bed and took all of his dirty laundry down to the basement to the laundry area for his mother to place it in the washer.

Next, he emptied all the trash from the trashcans throughout the house, placed it in a big plastic bag, and put the bag in the big can in the backyard.

Jeremy lived in a row home in West Philadelphia that had an open front porch. His job was to wash the porch with either a bucket containing water and a broom, or use the hose. Lastly, he had to sweep the sidewalk.

As he was finishing sweeping the sidewalk, his friend Jamal, who lived across the street, called his name. Jamal asked Jeremy if he wanted to go over to the schoolyard to shoot some hoops. Jeremy replied, "Not today," because he had something really important to do. Jamal then continued riding his bike in the direction of the schoolyard.

As he entered the house, his mother informed him that his little cousin, Kia, was coming over for a visit later that afternoon and would be spending the night. Kia was only six years old and she liked when Jeremy read stories to her. Jeremy was thinking that he was not going to have time for Kia today because he had something important to do.

Now that he had finished his chores, Jeremy went to look for Pop-Pop. He found him in his study reading the newspaper. As he entered the room, Pop-Pop asked if he was ready and Jeremy said, "Yes sir!"

Chapter 8 - Sergeant Isaac Brown

"Where were we, do you remember?" Pop-Pop asked. Jeremy said they had just started to talk about Isaac Brown. "Oh yes!" said Pop-Pop. "Sergeant Isaac Brown was your fifth great-grandfather."

On January 1, 1777, Isaac Brown enlisted as a sergeant in the 7th Virginia Regiment. He was approximately seventeen years of age. Boys as young as fourteen and men as old as forty-eight were mustered from Charles City County. Isaac, the youngest of Elizabeth Brown's sons, enlisted for the duration of the war. He was described as a farmer having black hair, black eyes, and a black complexion.

He began to open the big, leather binder. Jeremy stood up so that he could have a better view. Pop-Pop

showed him papers that had the words "muster roll" at the top and some had the words "pay roll" at the top. There was one of each for every month for years. Some had the words "enlisted for the duration of the war" on them. Sergeant Isaac Brown's name was on each sheet. The first was dated January 1, 1777, and the last April 5, 1783. Pop-Pop pointed out the pages showing Sergeant Isaac Brown was at Valley Forge with George Washington from March to May of 1778. Further in the binder, there were copies of Sergeant Isaac Brown's pension files, a letter from John Tyler, and a paper called a Last Will and Testament.

Jeremy was amazed. He asked his great-grandfather how he got all of this information. Pop-Pop told him about the special libraries where people can search colonial court records, wills, deeds, free Negro registers, marriage bonds, and military bonds. He mentioned libraries such as the National Archives in Washington, D.C., the David Library of the American Revolution in Washington Crossing, Pennsylvania, and those kept by historical societies.

Pay Roll	Muster Roll

Pay Roll

A | 11 | Va.

Isaac Brown

Sgt , { Capt. William Smith's Company in the 11th Virginia Reg't of Foot commanded by Lt. Col. John Cropper.

(Revolutionary War)

Appears on

Company Pay Roll

of the organization named above for the

month of _____ Apl _____ , 1778

Commencement of time _____ , 17

Commencement of pay _____ , 17

To what time paid _____ , 17

Pay per month _____ 8

Time of service From Apl to May 11 Month

Whole time of service _____

Subsistence _____

Amount of pay £2,58 _____

Amt. of pay and subsistence _____

Pay due to sick, absent _____

_____

Casualties: Sick in Camp _____

Remarks: _____

_____

_____

_____

_____

(545) A Douglas   Copyist

Muster Roll

B | 11 | Va.

Isaac Brown

Sgt , { Late Capt. William Smith's Co., 11th Virginia Reg't, commanded by Capt. Charles Porterfield.

(Revolutionary War.)

Appears on

Company Muster Roll

of the organization named above for the

month of _____ Mar _____ , 1778

Roll dated _ Valley Forge _____

_____ Apr 6 , 17

Appointed _____ , 17

Commissioned _____ , 17

Enlisted _____ , 17

Term of enlistment _____ War _____

Time since last muster or enlistment _____

Alterations since last muster _____

Casualties _____

Remarks: Sick in camp _____

_____

_____

(548) D. W. Woore   Copyist

National Archives of the United States.(1934). A Microfilm Publication, Film #16, reel 1021.

Pop-Pop went on to say, Sergeant Isaac Brown assisted in establishing American Independence while serving in the 7th, 11th and 15th Virginia Regiments of the Continental Line. He was in the battles of Guilford Courthouse, Siege of Fort Ninety-Six, and Eutaw Springs.

He went on to explain that during the months from December 1777 to June 1778 there was an encampment at Valley Forge in Pennsylvania where approximately 12,000 troops gathered, with 1,500 of the men being patriots of African descent. During this encampment, the weather was severe and the water was contaminated. Therefore, about 2,000 men died.

"Our grandfather, Sergeant Isaac Brown, was at Valley Forge with General Washington from March 1778 thru May 1778. He was sick but he survived. When the men marched into Valley Forge, they were fragmented, dejected, and feeling defeated. They marched out as a unified army with a military manual, military maneuvers, and confidence."

Several other Brown family members were involved in this cause:

Abram Brown—believed to have been an uncle enlisted in the 3rd Virginia Regiment: deserted after twenty-one days. He was too old.

Benjamin Brown—drafted but later deserted

Edward Brown—served in the state militia

Freeman Brown—served in the state militia

William Brown—served on the Continental Line

Abraham Brown—twice donated beef to the Continental Line

Dixon Brown—donated one pair of stillards or scales for Colonel Nicholas and the militia for the Continental Line

Jeremy could not believe his luck to be a part of history through his family. He bet Kia would be surprised too. His great-grandfather explained how he was a direct descendant of both Isaac and Abraham Brown. Isaac had a son named Carver and Carver married Rebecca who was the granddaughter of Abraham. She was actually his second-generation cousin.

Sergeant Isaac Brown, a non-commissioned officer, received a pension of $96 per year until his death. At the time of his death, Isaac Brown owned seventy-five acres of land abutting, Greenway, the property of the Tyler family. Jeremy saw a copy of Isaac Brown's Last Will and Testament in the leather binder.

Chapter 9 - All Black Colonial Units

Jeremy asked Pop-Pop when was the war over. Pop-Pop described that in the summer of 1781, the Continental Army consisted of about 6,000 men, one fourth, or 1,500, were men of color. The Marquis de Lafayette had arranged for his slave named James Armistead to serve as a double agent. He was hired by Lord Cornwallis to spy on the Americans. James Armistead reported to the Marquis that Cornwallis had begun fortifying at Yorktown.

There were three all-black colonial units: the 1st Rhode Island Regiment, the Second Company of the 4th Connecticut Regiment, and the Bucks of America. The Bucks of America were from Massachusetts and were under the command of Colonel George Middleton, the only black commissioned officer in the Continental Army. A fourth-all black unit traveled from Haiti with the French—the Black Brigade of Saint Dominique.

James Armistead

Marquis de Lafayette

The 1st Rhode Island Regiment joined Major General John Sullivan's division. At Yorktown, they were among the 4,300 men who dug the first parallel of trenches on October 6, 1781, five hundred yards from the enemy. They were in the trenches again on October 15, 1781 when Lord Cornwallis manned his serious Redoubts #9 and #10—fortifications against the French and Americans.

The French took Redoubt #9 and the 1st Rhode Island Regiment took Redoubt #10. Jeremy looked at his great-grandfather and asked, "Took them out?"

Pop-Pop replied, "Took them out! In fact, Redoubt #10 turned out to be the last major battle of the war."

Two days later, early in the afternoon on October 19, 1781, the British army and their German allies laid down their arms in defeat. Yorktown was destroyed. Corpses were everywhere.

Chapter 10 - The Best Story

The peace treaty that officially ended colonial rule was signed in 1783—the Paris Peace Treaty. The war had lasted for eight years.

Jeremy was thinking this was the best story that Pop-Pop had ever shared. He could not wait to go to school and tell Mrs. Woods and the class that he was a direct descendant of two patriots.

"Pop-Pop, should we tell the story to Kia?" Pop-Pop said Kia was only in the first grade and maybe they should wait until she was a little older. "But I will tell you what we can do. Following the four hundredth anniversary of the founding of the colony at Jamestown, a monument was unveiled at the Elam Baptist Church in Charles City County honoring the African Americans from Charles City that served in the Revolutionary War. We will take Kia with us to visit the monument and the church."

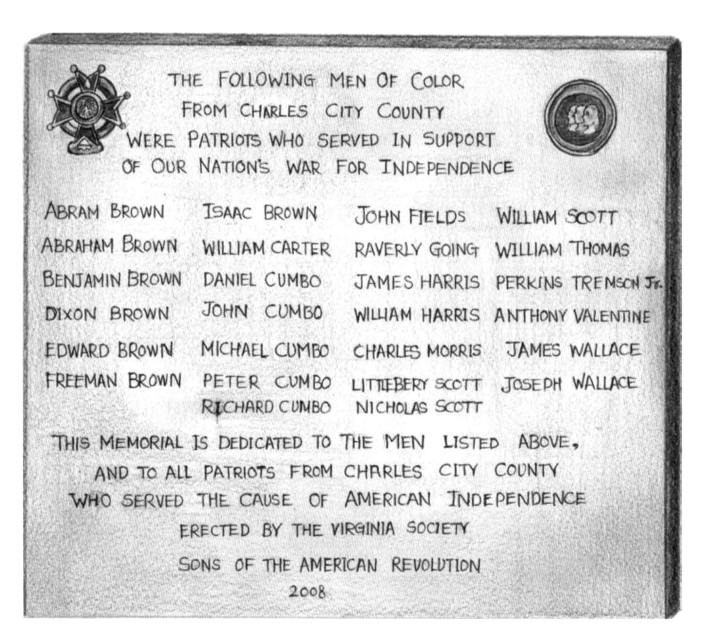

THE FOLLOWING MEN OF COLOR
FROM CHARLES CITY COUNTY
WERE PATRIOTS WHO SERVED IN SUPPORT
OF OUR NATION'S WAR FOR INDEPENDENCE

ABRAM BROWN	ISAAC BROWN	JOHN FIELDS	WILLIAM SCOTT
ABRAHAM BROWN	WILLIAM CARTER	RAVERLY GOING	WILLIAM THOMAS
BENJAMIN BROWN	DANIEL CUMBO	JAMES HARRIS	PERKINS TRENSON JR.
DIXON BROWN	JOHN CUMBO	WILLIAM HARRIS	ANTHONY VALENTINE
EDWARD BROWN	MICHAEL CUMBO	CHARLES MORRIS	JAMES WALLACE
FREEMAN BROWN	PETER CUMBO	LITTLEBERY SCOTT	JOSEPH WALLACE
	RICHARD CUMBO	NICHOLAS SCOTT	

THIS MEMORIAL IS DEDICATED TO THE MEN LISTED ABOVE,
AND TO ALL PATRIOTS FROM CHARLES CITY COUNTY
WHO SERVED THE CAUSE OF AMERICAN INDEPENDENCE
ERECTED BY THE VIRGINIA SOCIETY
SONS OF THE AMERICAN REVOLUTION
2008

51

Just then, Kia came running into the room asking, "Did I hear someone call me?"

"No," answered Pop-Pop, "but we sure are happy to see you! Where is my hug?" With that, Kia ran to give her Pop-Pop a big hug.

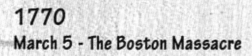

1770
March 5 - The Boston Massacre

1773
December 16 - The Boston Tea Party

1775
April 18 - The midnight ride of Paul Revere
April 19 - The Battle of Lexington and Concord
June 17 - The Battle of Bunker Hill (Breeds Hill)
July 3 - George Washington takes command of the Continental Army

1776
July 4 - The Continental Congress adopts the Declaration of Independence

1777
June 14 - Congress officially adopts the American flag
December 19 - The Continental Army arrives at Valley Forge

1778
February 6 - France signs the Treaty of Aid to help the colonies
June 19 - The Continental Army marches out of Valley Forge
July 10 - France declares war on England

1781
March 1 - The 13 states ratify the Articles of Confederation
October 19 - The British surrender at Yorktown
November 5 - John Hanson is elected the first President of
the United States

1783
February 14 - England officially declares an end to the war
September 3 - The United States and England sign the
Paris Peace Treaty
December 23 - George Washington officially resigns from his
command and returns to private life

Sources Consulted

Abercrombie, J. and L., R. Slatten. (1992). Index to the Virginia Revolutionary "Publick" Claims County Booklets. Athens, Georgia: Iberian Publishing Company.

Atlas of Historical County Boundaries. (2000). The Newberry Library. Retrieved January 6, 2011, from historical-county.newberry/virginia/viewer.htm

Blanco, R. L. (Ed.) *The American Revolution 1775–1783. Vol. II: M–Z.* New York: Garland Publishing, 1993.

Boatner, M. "The Negro in the Revolution." *American History Illustrated* 4(5), (1969): 36–44.

Charles City County. (2006). Revolutionary War Roster. Retrieved January 2, 2007, from charlescity.org.

Greene, R. E. *Black Courage.* Washington: National Society of the Daughters of the American Revolution, 1984.

Gwathmey, J. H. *Historical Register of Virginians in the Revolution.* Baltimore, Maryland: Genealogical Publishing Company, 1979.

Hartgrove, W.B. "The Negro Soldier in the American Revolution." *Journal of Negro History* 1(2), (1916): 110–131.

Heinegg, P. *Free African Americans of North Carolina, Virginia, and South Carolina* (5th ed.). Baltimore, Maryland: Clearfield, 2005.

Jackson, L. P. "Virginia Negro Soldiers and Seamen in the American Revolution." *Journal of Negro History* 27, (1942): 247–287.

Kaplan, S., and E. N. Kaplan. *The Black Presence in the Era of the American Revolution.* Amherst: University of Massachusetts Press, 1989.

Lanning, M. L. *Defenders of Liberty.* New York: Citadel Press, 2000.

National Archives of the United States. (1934). A Microfilm Publication, Film #16, reel 1021.

Puckrein, G. A. *The Black Regiment in the American Revolution*. Providence: Afro-American Studies Program Brown University and Rhode Island Black Heritage Society, 1978.

Quarles, B. *The Negro in the American Revolution*. New York: W. W. Norton & Company, 1973.

Whittenburg, J. P. (Ed.), and J. M. Coski (Ed.). *Charles City County Virginia: An Official History*. Salem, West Virginia: Don Mills, 1989.